Welcome to

Join Daisy and Tom on their Genie Street adventures by visiting them at Ladybird's Genie Street website.

Find out about the latest Genie Street books and meet all your favourite Lampland characters!

www.ladybirdgeniestreet.com

Written by Richard Dungworth

Illustrated by Sarah Horne

A catalogue record for this book is available from the British Library

Published by Ladybird Books Ltd.
A Penguin Company
Penguin Books Ltd., 80 Strand, London, WC2R 0RL
Penguin Books Australia Ltd., Camberwell, Victoria, Australia
Penguin Group (NZ) 67 Apollo Drive, Rosedale,
North Shore 0632, New Zealand

001 – 10 9 8 7 6 5 4 3 2 1

ISBN: 978-1-40931-239-0

Printed in Great Britain by Clays Ltd, St Ives plc

THIS LADYBIRD
BOOK BELONGS TO

Tom and Daisy live on Genie Street, with their mum and dad.

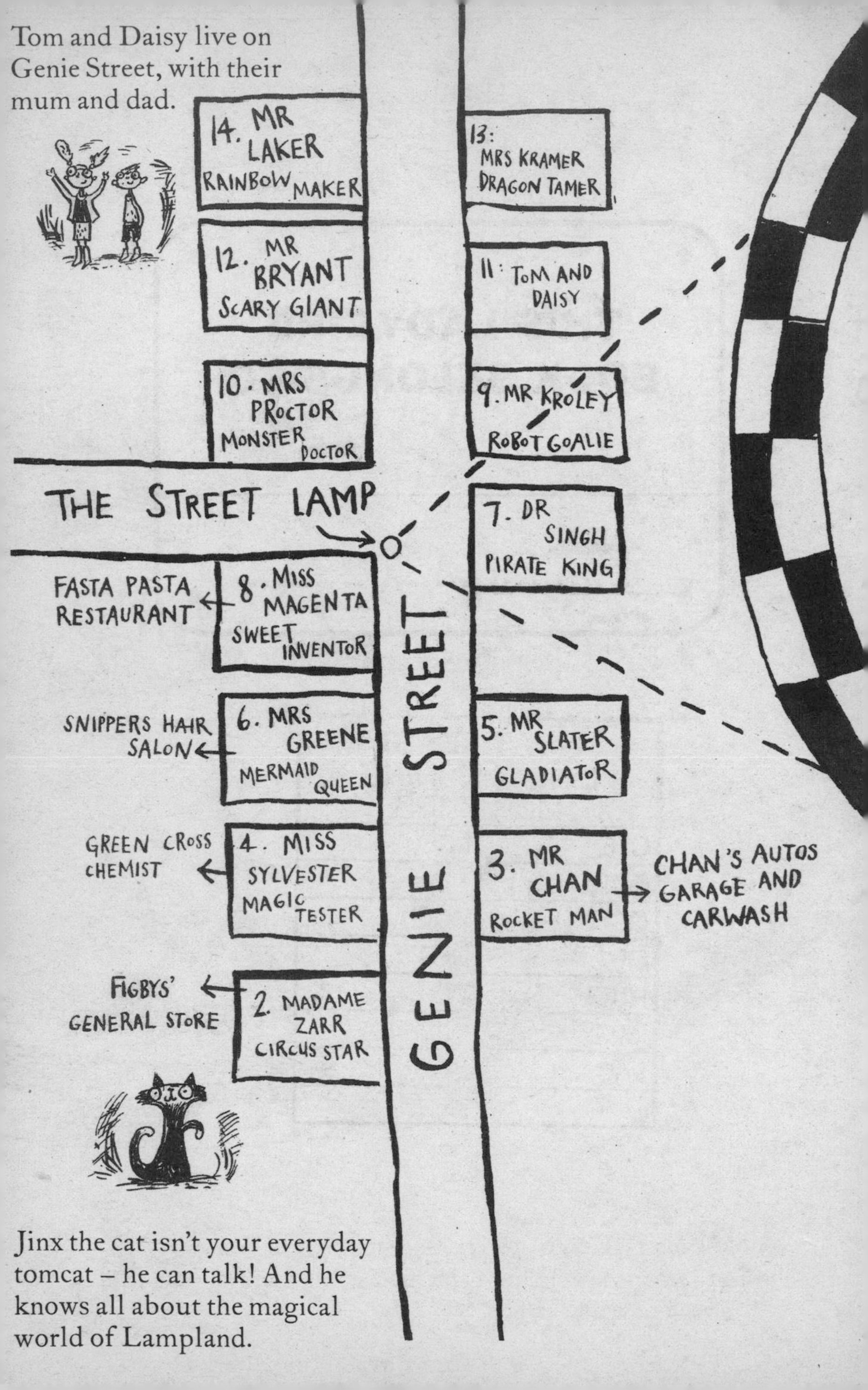

Jinx the cat isn't your everyday tomcat – he can talk! And he knows all about the magical world of Lampland.

Mr Mistry, Genie Street's postman, gives Tom and Daisy a special parcel which sends them on each new adventure!

Mrs Kramer
DRAGON TAMER

Contents

Chapter One
Moving In 9

Chapter Two
The Street Lamp 17

Chapter Three
Special Delivery 25

Chapter Four
Through the Door 33

Chapter Five
The Shiny Whistle 41

Chapter Six
Dragon Riders 51

Chapter Seven
Falling Home 59

Chapter One
Moving In

Tom and Daisy stood on the pavement and watched the removal van drive away.

'Well, that's that then,' said Daisy. She turned and looked at their new house. Mum and Dad were inside, already unpacking their stuff. 'We live here now. On Genie Street.'

Tom looked a bit fed up. He hadn't been very keen on moving.

'I hope there are *some* other children around here,' he said. He had just spotted an old lady looking out from a window next door. 'We're not going to have much fun otherwise, are we?'

A black and white cat was lying on a nearby wall. Daisy liked cats. She went over and began to stroke its ears gently.

'What do *you* think, Puss?' said Daisy. 'Is there anything exciting to do around here?'

The cat pushed against her hand and purred. It looked up at Daisy with yellow eyes.

'*Exciting*?' said the cat. 'Oh, yes. Absolutely.'

Daisy's hand froze. She stared at the cat. She hadn't expected it to answer. Tom looked stunned, too.

The cat jumped down from the wall. It looked up at Daisy again.

'The secret,' it purred, 'is knowing where to look.'

Chapter Two

The Street Lamp

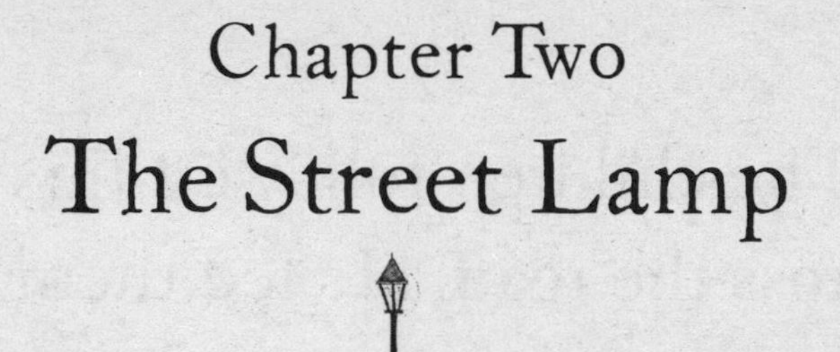

The black and white cat began to walk across the road.

Tom looked at Daisy. 'Did that cat just...?'

The cat looked back over its shoulder. 'Yes, I did,' it purred. 'And the name is Jinx, by the way – not "Puss" or "that cat". Now, come along. I have something to show you.'

The children followed Jinx across the road. He led them towards the row of shops near the end of the street. He stopped at the base of an ordinary street lamp.

'There!' said Jinx. He looked up at the street lamp as though it was very special indeed.

'There *what*?' said Tom.

'Watch closely!' said Jinx.

He began to rub his furry body against the lamp post. First he stretched up tall, then he crouched down low.

'*Once up… once down…*' purred Jinx. '*Then three times round and round…*'

He moved slowly round the post – once… twice… three times…

And then something *very* odd happened.

The street lamp lit up very brightly. It had a magical purple glow. A moment later, a ball of sparkling light shot out from the lamp. Tom and Daisy watched it go fizzing across the street. The street lamp went out again.

'What's happening, Jinx?' cried Daisy.

But Jinx had vanished.

Chapter Three
Special Delivery

Tom and Daisy hurried to see where the strange ball of light had gone. It had struck the front door of the house next to theirs. They could see that the number on the door was glowing purple.

'Hullo, hullo!'

Both children jumped at the sound of a voice behind them.

The voice belonged to a short plump man with a very jolly face. He was wearing a smart purple uniform, and he was on a bike. It was strange that they hadn't heard him coming.

'Special Delivery!' beamed the little man. He passed Daisy a small parcel wrapped in brown paper.

'Are you the postman?' asked Tom. 'We're new here, you see.'

'Then welcome to Genie Street!' said the man in purple. 'Mr Mistry, at your service! Special Deliveries only!' He pointed to the parcel. 'And that one is *very* special, bless my ears!'

Tom and Daisy looked at the parcel. They read the address on it.

MRS
KRAMER,
13 GENIE ST,
PIPTON

'So, do you want *us* to give this to Mrs Kramer?' asked Tom.

There was no reply. The children looked up. Mr Mistry had gone.

'Wow!' said Daisy. 'He's quick on that bike of his, isn't he?' She looked back at the parcel. 'I suppose he *must* want us to deliver this. Come on!'

Chapter Four
Through the Door

Daisy and Tom walked up to Mrs Kramer's front door. There was a door-knocker on it. It had a purple glow, like the house number.

Daisy meant to bang the door-knocker three times. But, the moment she touched it, things went crazy.

There was a dazzling burst of purple light. The world tipped upside down. For a few seconds, Tom and Daisy felt like they were falling – right through the door in front of them.

And then suddenly it was over. Everything went back to normal.

Except they weren't on Genie Street any more.

'What happened?' said Daisy. 'Where are we?'

Tom was looking around in amazement, too. They were on a hilltop, near a forest. There was a building in the distance.

'That looks a lot like a castle!' said Tom. 'And it has flags flying!'

The air felt suddenly cool. A shadow passed over them.

'Daisy, look!' said Tom. 'Isn't that Mrs Kramer?'

The old lady from next door was running up the hill towards them. She was waving her arms and yelling.

'What's she so worked up about?' said Daisy.

A huge, angry-looking dragon landed on the hillside.

'Er... maybe *that*!' croaked Tom.

Chapter Five
The Shiny Whistle

Mrs Kramer reached the hilltop, huffing and puffing.

'Don't panic!' she wheezed. 'Stand back! I'm a fully trained Dragon Tamer! I deal with deadly fire-breathing creatures like this one every day!'

She reached into her handbag and pulled out a tiny shiny whistle.

The dragon started to move closer. Wisps of smoke came from its nostrils.

Tom felt that he probably *should* panic.

'How are you going to stop it with a *whistle*?' he asked Mrs Kramer.

'This isn't just *any* whistle,' replied Mrs Kramer. 'It's a very special Dragon Taming one. Watch!'

Mrs Kramer put the whistle to her lips and blew.

The whistle made a very rude noise.

The dragon ignored it completely.

'Oh dear!' said Mrs Kramer. She looked as worried as Tom and Daisy now. 'It shouldn't sound like that at all! It must have got a little melted when I last used it.'

Daisy felt something rub against her leg. She looked down. 'Jinx!'

The black and white cat was weaving round her feet.

'What are you doing here?' asked Daisy.

'Nothing in particular,' purred Jinx. 'Although I did wonder if this might be a good moment to remind you about a certain *very special* delivery…'

'Oh! Yes!' cried Daisy. She had forgotten all about Mr Mistry's parcel. She quickly gave it to Mrs Kramer.

Mrs Kramer tore off the brown paper. Inside it was another whistle.

The dragon was very close now. It let out a terrifying roar.

Mrs Kramer answered with a blast on her new whistle.

Chapter Six
Dragon Riders

The dragon stopped roaring. It lay down, tucked in its wings and rolled on to its back.

Tom and Daisy were amazed to see Mrs Kramer walk right up to the dragon. She started stroking its tummy. The dragon made happy snorting noises.

'Now *that's* more like it!' said Mrs Kramer.

'He's as gentle as a pussycat now!' Mrs Kramer smiled.

Jinx gave her a hard stare.

Mrs Kramer blew another short blast on her whistle. The dragon rolled over again. It stayed crouched on the ground.

'Anyone for a dragon ride?' asked Mrs Kramer.

Moments later, Tom and Daisy found themselves doing something they had never dreamt of.

They were soaring through the air on the back of a huge red dragon.

Far below, they could see mountains, forests, lakes and castles.

'Lampland looks very beautiful from up here, doesn't it, my dears?' said Mrs Kramer.

'Lampland?' yelled Tom. He had to shout over the rushing wind. 'Is that where we are then?'

'Yes!' Mrs Kramer replied. 'And it's a wonderful, magical place, believe me!'

'Will we be able to get back home?' asked Daisy.

'Oh yes, my dear!' said Mrs Kramer. 'In fact, look there – just up ahead...'

Chapter Seven
Falling Home

Up ahead was a patch of sky that looked odd. It shimmered and had a purple tinge.

'That's our way home!' yelled Mrs Kramer. She steered the dragon so that it flew right over the shimmering patch. With a cry of '*Geronimo*!', she jumped off the dragon's back.

Jinx leapt after her.

Tom and Daisy looked at each other. There was nothing else for it. They crossed their fingers and jumped.

'Whhhhoooooa!' yelled Daisy.

'Aaaaarrrrggghhh!' cried Tom.

The air rushed past them. The shimmering patch of sky raced up to meet them…

And then they were standing on Genie Street, outside Mrs Kramer's door.

'Tom! Daisy! Come inside and help with some of this unpacking!' Dad was calling from an upstairs window next door.

Mrs Kramer smiled at them. 'Here, my dears…' She passed Daisy her old whistle. 'You two can keep this. It might still work on *small* dragons.'

'*Now*, please!' shouted Dad.

Mrs Kramer winked. 'Or even on grown-ups,' she said.

13

Tom and Daisy quickly said goodbye to Mrs Kramer.

As they went indoors, Tom smiled to himself.

'I reckon life on Genie Street is going to be more fun than I thought,' he told his sister. 'A *lot* more fun...'

Mr Laker
RAINBOW MAKER

Contents

Chapter One
That Cat Again 69

Chapter Two
The Street Lamp's Choice 77

Chapter Three
Back to Lampland 85

Chapter Four
Mr Laker's Problem 93

Chapter Five
Rainbow Paint 101

Chapter Six
Hover Sweets 109

Chapter Seven
Imp Trouble 115

Chapter Eight
Rainbow's End 121

Chapter One
That Cat Again

Tom and Daisy woke up for the first time in their new house on Genie Street. They both had the same thought.

'It *can't* have been real, can it?' said Daisy. The day before, they had shared a magical adventure. There had been a dragon in it. And a talking cat called Jinx.

'But cats can't talk,' said Daisy. 'Can they?'

'There's only one way to find out!' said Tom.

They went to look for Jinx. They soon found him, snoozing in the morning sun.

Jinx opened one yellow eye. He stretched out his front legs and yawned.

'Ah,' he purred. 'The dragon-riders. Good morning.'

'So it *was* real!' cried Daisy. 'We really *did* go to Lampland!'

Tom's eyes sparkled. 'Can we go back?' he asked. 'Can you make the street lamp's magic work again?'

'*Please*, Jinx!' begged Daisy.

Jinx still had one eye closed. He yawned again.

'I'm rather busy at the moment,' he said. 'But there's no reason why you shouldn't rub the lamp yourselves.'

'Mind you,' Jinx went on, 'you can't just rub it any-old-how. Remember –

Once up,
Once down,
Then three times
Round and round.'

'Got it!' said Tom.

'Splendid,' purred Jinx. 'Now, I really *must* get back to what I was doing.'

And he closed his eye again.

Chapter Two

The Street Lamp's Choice

Tom and Daisy crossed the road and hurried towards the shops. They stopped at the street lamp outside Fasta Pasta.

'Shall I try?' Daisy asked Tom. 'Or do you want to?'

'No, you go on,' said Tom.

Daisy put her hand on the lamp post. It felt warm.

'*Once up...*' muttered Daisy. She raised her hand, rubbing the lamp gently. '*Once down...*'

'Now you have to rub *around* it!' Tom reminded her.

Daisy remembered. '*Then three times round and round...*' she chanted.

She finished her third circle round the street lamp. Her fingers began to tingle.

The street lamp lit up, bright purple.

'It's working!' cried Daisy.

A ball of light shot out from the lamp. It flew straight up the street a little way, then swerved to the left. It hit the door of a house further along the same side of the street.

'Come on!' said Tom.

ER
&
14

The magic street lamp had chosen the house at Number 14. The house number was glowing purple. So was the doorbell.

'Shall I ring it?' Tom asked Daisy.

Before she could reply, somebody else spoke.

'Not so fast, bless my ears!'

The children spun round.

14

Chapter Three
Back to Lampland

'Hello, Mr Mistry!' said Daisy.

'Hullo, hullo!' grinned the little man. He was in the same purple uniform as when the children had last met him. But today he was on a scooter. Mr Mistry pulled a parcel from his purple sack. It seemed rather too large to have fitted inside.

'Special Delivery for Mr Laker!' said Mr Mistry.

He passed the parcel to Tom. It was quite heavy.

'What is it?' asked Tom.

'Surprise supplies!' sang Mr Mistry. 'A little something for his work!' He pointed to the van parked on the street. The children read what was on it.

J.T.LAKER
PAINTER &
DECORATOR

'So, do you want –'

Daisy broke off. There was no point asking Mr Mistry anything. He wasn't there any more.

Tom whistled. 'That's one super-fast scooter!' he said.

He looked at the parcel. Then he looked back at the glowing doorbell.

'Come on!' he said. 'Let's see if Mr Laker is in!'

14

Tom reached for the bell. He pressed it.

'Whhhooooaaaa!' cried Daisy.

The world seemed to start spinning. The children were dazzled by a blaze of purple light. The ground lurched suddenly, and they felt themselves falling forward.

And then they were standing in a peaceful green meadow that was full of flowers.

Chapter Four

Mr Laker's Problem

Tom and Daisy noticed two things almost at once.

The first thing was a huge, beautiful rainbow. Or rather *part* of a rainbow. It arched up from the meadow, but stopped in mid-air. Its colours were so bright they made Daisy gasp.

The second thing was the van parked among the flowers.

The children hurried over to the van. They could hear someone muttering behind it.

'Oh dear, oh dear! What a mess! Wait till I get my hands on them! Why, I'll –'

The van's rear doors were wide open. A man was looking into the back of the van in dismay. He looked up in surprise at Tom and Daisy.

'Hello!' said Daisy. 'I'm Daisy. And this is Tom. Are you Mr Laker?'

The man nodded.

Tom was staring inside the van. It really was in a mess. There were decorating tools and paint everywhere.

'What happened?'

'Imps!' said Mr Laker. 'The little pests got in while I was busy painting my rainbow!'

'You paint rainbows?' said Daisy in amazement.

Mr Laker nodded proudly.

'Make 'em and paint 'em!' he said. 'Every rainbow in Lampland!'

His smile faded. He looked at the part-painted rainbow.

'Only I won't be finishing *this* one,' he said sadly. 'Those wretched imps have spilled every last drop of my Rainbow Paint!'

Chapter Five
Rainbow Paint

'Don't worry, Mr Laker!' said Daisy. 'I have a feeling we might have the answer to your problem!' She gave Tom a look.

'Oh! Of course!' cried Tom. 'Mr Mistry's Special Delivery!'

He quickly handed the heavy parcel to Mr Laker.

Inside the parcel was a large tin of Rainbow Paint.

'Marvellous!' cried Mr Laker.

He looked thoughtful for a moment or two.

'I wonder,' he said at last. 'Could you lend me a hand, perhaps? If you two finished painting the rainbow, I could make a start on tidying my van.'

'Of course!' said Tom and Daisy together.

Mr Laker poured some Rainbow Paint from the big tin into two smaller pots. Then, he found Tom and Daisy a brush each.

Tom peered at his paint.

'But... it's just plain *white*,' he said. 'How can we paint a rainbow with this?'

Mr Laker grinned. 'Give it a try!' he said.

Tom went over to the unfinished end of the rainbow. He began brushing on paint from his pot.

The paint looked white on Tom's brush. But, as he spread it over the rainbow, its colour changed. It made perfect stripes of red, orange, yellow, green, blue, indigo and violet.

'Cool!' cried Daisy, and she hurried to help.

Chapter Six
Hover Sweets

The children worked their way along the rainbow. Soon they were painting on tiptoe.

'Do you have a ladder?' Tom shouted to Mr Laker.

'I've got something better than that!' said Mr Laker. He took a bag of stripy sweets from his pocket. He gave one to Tom and one to Daisy.

Tom and Daisy exchanged puzzled looks.

'How will a sweet help us reach higher?' asked Tom.

Mr Laker smiled. 'Suck it and see!' he replied.

The children did as they were told. They popped their sweets into their mouths and began to suck.

The sweets tasted lovely. But that wasn't all…

'I'm floating!' cried Daisy.

'Me, too!' yelled Tom.

Their feet had left the ground. As they sucked their sweets, they rose higher into the air. The harder they sucked, the faster they climbed.

'Hover Sweets!' Mr Laker yelled up at them. 'Great, aren't they?'

Tom and Daisy were soon painting away happily again, high in the sky.

Chapter Seven

Imp Trouble

Daisy had been painting for a while when she happened to look down. She gave Tom a nudge. 'Look!' she whispered.

Below them, two very small, very green figures were sneaking through the long meadow grass. They were heading for the tin of Rainbow Paint.

'Imps?' hissed Tom.

'I guess so!' replied Daisy.

The imps hadn't noticed Tom and Daisy up in the air. The children decided to teach them a lesson. They stopped sucking their Hover Sweets. They dropped from the sky like stones, and landed right in front of the sneaking imps.

'Boogly-boogly-boo!' yelled Daisy, waving her arms.

'Mwa-ha-haaaa!' wailed Tom, pulling a face.

The imps were scared out of their wits. They turned and ran.

Mr Laker came over. He was laughing.

'Nice work, you two!' he said. 'They'll be from the Fairy Forest.' He pointed to some woodland in the distance. 'It's full of imps and sprites. They're only happy when they're up to mischief. But those two won't be back in a hurry!'

Chapter Eight
Rainbow's End

Tom and Daisy finished painting the rainbow without any more imp trouble.

'Wonderful job!' beamed Mr Laker. 'Thank you so much! Now, you two had better get home. Here –'

He gave Tom and Daisy two more Hover Sweets each.

'Put both in at once and suck as hard as you can!'

Tom and Daisy sucked the magical stripy sweets. They began to rise into the air again.

They sucked harder… and climbed faster… and faster!

Soon they were shooting upwards like rockets.

'Yee-hah!' yelled Tom.

'Bye-bye, Mr Laker!' cried Daisy. Then their ears popped and there was a blinding flash of purple light.

They were back on Genie Street, outside Number 14.

Tom looked at Daisy. His sister's eyes were as wide as his.

'Wow!' said Tom. 'That was *some* ride!'

Daisy nodded. Then she looked puzzled. 'There's something in my pocket,' she said.

She pulled out a wrapped Hover Sweet.

14

Tom found another Hover Sweet in his pocket, too.

'Mr Laker must have slipped them in,' said Daisy.

'I'm going to save mine for a rainy day,' said Tom. He grinned. 'Or even another *rainbow* day!'

Daisy smiled back. Then they set off to find Jinx and tell him all about it.

GENIE S
LAKER
INTER &
DECORATOR

Parent note

Genie Street is a brand new fiction series that is the next step up from Ladybird's Read it yourself Level 4. Ideal for newly independent Key Stage 1 readers, these books are for children who want to read real fiction for the first time.

Collect all the titles in the series:

9781409312390

9781409312406

9781409312413

9781409312420

9781409312437

9781409312444

Each book contains two easy-to-read stories that children will love. The stories include short chapters, simple vocabulary and a clear layout that will encourage and build confidence when reading.